T0354685

THE PERFECT WITNESS

BONUS MATERIAL

LOGAN SNARE

iUniverse

THE PERFECT WITNESS
BONUS MATERIAL

iUniverse books may be ordered through
booksellers or by contacting:

iUniverse
1663 Liberty Drive
Bloomington, IN 47403
www.iuniverse.com
844-349-9409

ISBN: 978-1-6632-6635-4 (sc)
ISBN: 978-1-6632-6636-1 (e)

Print information available on the last page.

iUniverse rev. date: 11/07/2024

"THE PERFECT WITNESS: BONUS MATERIAL"
[GAG REELS AND DELETED SCENES]

CONTENTS

AUTHOR'S STATEMENT:

This is a companion to "THE PERFECT WITNESS: SCREENPLAY".
It is the "BONUS MATERIAL" and is "GAG REELS AND DELETED
SCENES", that includes a conversion of the manuscript
into a script format to introduce a variety of options
for roles: Lead Characters, Supporting Roles and Extras.
Additional roles are disclosed in the "BONUS MATERIAL"
for the "SCREENPLAY" and "COMING ATTRACTIONS" which is
to be released in conjunction with the Full Manuscript.
The format of this document is subjective and does not
in any way represent the actual manner by which the
story plays out in film. This work is broken down into
sections and each are listed numerically as BONUS #01-10
and "COMING ATTRACTIONS" for the "SCREENPLAY".

EDITOR'S NOTE:

Keynote: "You never know what's just around the corner."

Author Biography: Logan Snare is a brand label, which is a business title for a production corporation. My name is Abigail L. Stanwood. I am a documentary photographer. I hold a BFA and was voted among the top one hundred artists of the past 100 years in Boston, MA. I live and work in Los Angeles, CA. My current employment is under two people who worked in the Film and Music Industry. One employer was a director on the board the founded the Grammy's (The Recording Academy) and who served 6 terms as a director. And one employer worked in Hollywood in Publicity from the 1940's – 1960. He attended the Oscar's (Academy of Motion Picture Arts and Sciences) multiple times for work.

"Her writing [in the depiction of the Antagonist Villain] is delusional." - Community Health Centers of America

"She [in the depiction of the Medical Examiner] is judged to be of above average intelligence." - APA

Back Cover Copy: In 1989, a missing woman is found dead.

Investigators go to her apartment and find nothing. They are left without a clue. Twenty years later, the father of two children discovers the body of a murder victim.

Somehow, these deaths are related, and detectives soon get a break with the help of an old cold case.

In the midst of all this horror, a wandering husband is brought back to his wife. A traffic accident brings unexpected love to a man in need of a change. However, the killer is still out there and soon has an encounter with the happy new couple.

A major historic event is on the way, and a killer needs to be caught. Will the victims ever be laid to rest, or will a murderer continue to walk free?

                    BONUS #01 "BREAKING NEWS"

                         THE SPECIALIST [V.O.]
                    You make mistakes when you're
                    tired.

INT. DOWNTOWN STATION - DAY

A message from the county and city comes in that there's
a sign and notification for the access roads to be
closed. A "NO ACCESSS" Regional alert hazard message for
residents to be aware of weather danger is sent through
the emergency alert system.

The Lead Officer is not at the site. ANDREW IS in the
office annex waiting for the family to arrive and is
highlighting paperwork reports with a green marker. He
gets the call from those who have evaluated somatic
evidence at the site that's been picked up by another
innovation in the forensic department where somatic
evidence that is retrieved is immediately evaluated and
analyzed. The MEDICAL EXAMINER goes back to the precinct.

THE BEST MAN provides ANDREW with a new password to
access a locked account. ANDREW leaves the precinct to
go to the site by unmarked police vehicle.

MATTHEW arrives at the precinct. MELODY leaves the
precinct at the same time that ELIZABETH the MEDICAL
EXAINER leaves the precinct. They both arrive at
different times. The TABLOID NEWS station channel is
responsible for the data leak that is modeled after
BRUCE. The regional alert dispatch code error recognition
is related to that data leak.

INT. DOWNTOWN PRECINCT - DAY

The forensic message (d-02) on display from the content
of the debris at the site.

FIRST RESPONDER M-01
Two children. Their father
discovered the body of the
murder victim.

CAPTAIN [V.O.]
Did anyone identify the victim?

FIRST RESPONDER M-01
(reads dispatch)
No. Not yet

CAPTAIN
This message is an error.

FIRST RESPONDER M-01
An error correction message
has been sent out.

CAPTAIN
Good.

THE BEST MAN
LIEUTENANT. CHIEF. Stop.

CHIEF
I can't believe this system
error went through.

LIEUTENANT
You see it here.

THE BEST MAN
How could they miss it?

CADET #5
I didn't realize my hand hit
"2" instead of the "1" during
the data entry.

CONTINUED

                         CAPTAIN
                (stern face)
                Looks like someone sent out
                the error correction already.

ANDREW, incredulous. . .

                         ANDREW
                This kind of error message
                report getting sent? That's
                what it took for them to get
                their act together?

                         CADET #5
                Sorry

                         CAPTAIN
                It's okay. Next time follow
                protocol.

EXT. INVESTIGATION SITE - DAY

He calls out. . .

                         MATTHEW
                It's her. I know it's her. She's
                the one who went missing,

REGIONAL NEWS, fastidious, and TABLOID NEWS (b-05), stop.

MOUNTED OFFICER 2 canters up to them and does not
dismount. She gestures a motion for PARAMEDIC 1 to not
do the same.

The MEDICAL EXAMINER, confused, looks to the bright
phone screen, the HEAD MEDICAL EXAMINER who nods his
approval with a short message service reply.

The MEDICAL EXAMINER'S knees barely touch the ground
as MEDICAL EXAMINER ASSISTANT accepts his message in a
encrypted message application.

                                           CONTINUED

[CUT AWAY]

                    MEDICAL EXAMINER ASSISTANT
                    (accepts message)
                    I doubt you could have known sir.

                     THE HEAD MEDICAL EXAMINER
                    You saw it also.

                     MEDICAL EXAMINER ASSISTANT
                    How could they do that?

[END CUT AWAY]

INT. NEWS STATION CHANNEL - DAY

                         NEWS ANCHOR M-01
                    Huh?

                         NEWS ANCHOR F-01
                    (looks at prompt)
                    Okay. It looks like we have
                    breaking news

                         NEWS ANCHOR M-02
                    I can't believe they notified
                    the public before the family

                         NEWS ANCHOR M-03
                    How do you know that

                         NEWS ANCHOR F-02
                    Public information. we contacted
                    them for comment.

                         NEWS ANCHOR M-01
                    Disturbing.

                         NEWS ANCHOR M-04
                    Very.

                                          CONTINUED

                    NEWS ANCHOR F-03
          Lets cut to advertisement.

                    NEWS ANCHOR F-04
          (camera trains)
          Back in 90 seconds with a word
          from our sponsor.

                    NEWS ANCHOR M-02
          Geez. That's not what the
          statement said. (b-01)

                    ADVERTISING SPONSOR
          (DNC excerpt)

                    THE SITTING PRESIDENT
          You Need to Vote!

                    NEWS ANCHOR M-01
          Great. And we're back!

                    NEWS ANCHOR F-04
          Weather coming up.

                    NEWS ANCHOR M-04
          And in other news. . .

                    NEWS STATION CHANNEL
          And now, we return you to our
          regular programming.

PROVERB FEATURE (a-01):

Our vision changes at night. Part of that ability to see
is determined by rods and cones in our vision. It also is
related to the neurobiology of our brain. Some research
has shown that animals can sense things in a way that
is different than humans. For humans, we experience a
heightened sense in one regard when we lose another
sense. For example, one person who can't see might hear
sounds or smell in a more proficient manner than another

                                        CONTINUED

person. The proverb theme is associated with Murphy's Law and about animals mimicking sounds (animals that lead away other animals from their nest by mimicking the sounds of their own).

CONTINUED

BONUS #02 "DOUBLE TAKE"

Image. For the forensic retrieval process MELODY brings
a dispatch print on the tablet of the scan from the
initial attempt bodies submerged under water idea it's
an innovation. ANDREW is seen with a piece of paper in
his hand and it is the image that is subjective it could
be a sonogram of the body that is submerged in water the
forensic scanner is able to reticulate a scan in water
the same way that a dog can smell scent in water. (d-
11) I like the idea of how without her there is clatter
and hustle bustle some people say that the music starts
when their loved one arrives. But with her to him, time
stands still. For both of them. Time stands still.

The water in the river is moving fast and its really
rapid. You can see striation lines of alternating light
surfaces on top of the disturbed surface. The rain is
falling in a flash flood.

                    MELODY
          Wait. . . you did not file the
          paperwork.

ANDREW smiles. . .

MELODY touches his hand.

                    ANDREW
          I have just the thing.

EXT. INVESTIGATION SITE PERIMETER - DAY

                    MOUNTED OFFICER #1
          Hear that? The sound of the
          dogs.

MOUNTED OFFICER #1, (Asian, 30's) renews her station, but
MOUNTED OFFICER #2 (White, 40's) counters in response to
the untenable dispatch barrage.

The barking closer.

                                        CONTINUED

In disbelief...

MOUNTED OFFICER #1, furious, trots high to cut off
MOUNTED OFFICER #2 but her horse's foot slips in a puddle
of dirt and coagulate. She pulls back too high again,
but. . .

MOUNTED OFFICER #2 canters under and steps upwards into
MOUNTED OFFICER #1's exposed side. Unfortunately, not
enough to inhibit the slumping action.

MOUNTED OFFICER #1, stunned, backs away and looks at the
ground. She's never been in a situation like this before.
The horse angrily whinnies out of control.

MOUNTED OFFICER #2, sternly, avoids and side passes. . .

                    MOUNTED OFFICER #2
               (the rain begins)
               The weather report told me
               that –

                    MOUNTED OFFICER #1
               There would be rain?

                    MOUNTED OFFICER #2
               There would be rain.

EXT. DOWNTOWN STATION – DAY

THE MESSENGER, haughty, avoids an eye at THE SPECIALIST

EXT. INVESTIGATION SITE - DAY

                    MITCH 02
               Shh. Take her to the other K-9's.

As the K-9 DOG A-01 is led away, MITCH 02 without
looking...

                                                   CONTINUED

> MITCH 02
> Where is the K-9 PUPPY.

EXT. INVESTIGATION SITE: EMBANKMENT - DAY

Two focused men, preoccupied and white, exit the site
on foot while two women rush to the site.

Prepared for SECOND AIRLIFT ATTEMPT #2, they have no
idea their timing is staggered because of an accident.

One woman wears a hat upon her head. She is MELODY.

> FIRST RESPONDER 05
> Bring me the hitch and binding.
> Don't do anything with the
> rest.

> The pine needles begin to fall.

EXT. INVESTIGATION SITE: TREE LINE - DAY

Muffled sounds of K-9 DOG A-01. The muted whine of the
K-9 PUPPY... then a puppy erratically digs.

Two bodies lie where discovered. Their bodies and
presentation both distinct and separate by their age
and location.

MELODY calmly adjusts the visor on her head in front of
the kneeling ANDREW and K-9 DOG A-01.

ANDREW struggles to contain his fear.

FIRST RESPONDER 03, obstinate...

> FIRST RESPONDER 05
> Who are you men?

                                           CONTINUED

                      FIRST RESPONDER 04
            And why were those two men
            directed to leave?

                          MELODY
            Recognizes, nods to a man
            behind ANDREW who suddenly
            renders FIRST RESPONDER 02 and
            FIRST RESPONDER 01 to pull back
            the top soil where K-9 PUPPY
            is digging.

K-9 DOG A-02, steadfast, approaches and whimpers softly.

MELODY nods to ANDREW...

                        ANDREW
            Put him with MITCH 02.

He motions FIRST RESPONDER 03 and FIRST RESPONDER 05 to
him as two men drag the excess soil away...

CONTINUED

BONUS #03 "THE CONCERT"

There are laws that govern conduct. And those laws
represent rules and regulations that are set for and
put in place for a reason.

When you are on the street there is no classification
unless otherwise indicated. What constitutes as public
property depends on the region. In the United States of
America public intersections that have crosswalks also
have security cameras. The cameras, which are normally
positioned on top of the traffic light structures
document what is happening on a day to day basis. The
footage is kept for anywhere between 24-72 hours to 30
or 40 days, depending on the region and state.

INT. CLUB VENUE - NIGHT

                    SECURITY BOUNCER 02
               (blocks with arm)
               No.

                         ATTENDEE #2
               Huh?

                    SECURITY BOUNCER 02
               No. Come back when you're a
               size 0.

There's a certain area where people are allowed to walk
on the floor of most venues. Things in life are separated
into classes. If you are in the first class (the "A-List")
you must adhere to a certain standard of dress and
conduct. And if you are in a lower class the requirements
are less, although they do still comprise of such.

                         ATTENDEE #2
               (turns around)
               He said "come back when you're
               a size 0."

                                        CONTINUED

> SECURITY BOUNCER 01
> I guess you're going to have to
> come back.

EXT. BROWNSTONE - DAY

> AGING COUPLE MALE
> When you go into a room
> after you sign a contract the
> people who own the place own
> everything you say. And that's
> why you need to be careful.

Now these two live in the same area as the apartment
complex where everything is happening. This is before
when she says "Who are all these people" and "we don't
usually stay here this time of year." This is the time
where we see him eating chips and drinking his single
malt and she is in the other room while reading the
newspaper extending her legs.

The raid physically impacts the building that the aging
couple reside in and there are workers who have to
go down this alley that leads around the side of the
building because of this area that's crumbling. "We
don't usually stay here this late in the season," the
AGING COUPLE FEMALE says to a young man outside. "We're
going to be leaving soon anyway." And then the AGING
COUPLE FEMALE goes inside. "What are all these people
doing here?" She says to her husband. "We told you," he
says. The AGING COUPLE MALE says, "We told you, they came
here and told us that they were going to be here today."
There's crashing in the in the distance because of what's
happening next door and the workers are going through
the alley that partitions one building from the other.
She stands there with both hands on her hips. "That's
it," She says. "I'm going back to Kingman." Something
that happens in the future of the story is presented
at the beginning. Outside a blue vehicle drives by the
front of the building with a young man driving, who is
a typical modern guy and he's driving in one direction
past other vehicles on the street after the heat of
the day. It is the image of the way it feels in the

CONTINUED

summertime when the sun is setting and the day is warm
and into establish the time of year.

That guy who drives by is the guy that VERONICA had
been seeing he's the guy from work he's also the guy
from work, JAMES, who was cheating on his girlfriend,
HALEY, with VERONICA, but he doesn't know that she was
murdered. Nobody knows because her body hadn't been
found yet. JAMES is going to be the one to report her
missing 3 days after she disappears. Nobody knows where
she is, and it's not that nobody cares -- -- it's just
that people have their own lives and right now his life
is bringing him, JAMES, to his girlfriend, HALEY, whose
parents live in the rural area of that region near the
river. You have to drive through the woods a little bit
you have to that's where you can see the prominence of
the trees that are in that area and how vast and quiet
it is yet there are many houses over in that region.

HANK and CARLA they live nearby as well. This big river
draws through the region of this part of the state and
it leads to other red rivers that do connect to the ocean
in Manhattan now Long Island and Manhattan are for sake
of the story about an hour and a half, you can take a
really fast train and then drive there's a high-speed.
Carla takes the high-speed train in the afternoon in
order to get to New York that morning she took a train
that was just a basic hour or so into the city. HANK
drops her off with the kids, and then he drops the kids
off at school and then he goes back home.

INT. BROWNSTONE APARTMENT - DAY

THE AGING COUPLE MALE AND FEMALE are both in the TV
Room and the fan is on. His wife is trying to set up a
shade to inhibit the bright light that shines into the
room through a window on the ceiling, a skylight. They
are waiting for people to arrive. Their caregiver is in
the kitchen.

THE AGING COUPLE MALE, his hand on his TV remote, glares
at the shadow of a bird in his peripheral vision in
the window. When he looks away the bird disappears. He
turns back and the bird peers inside its beak against

CONTINUED

the window pane. Like the jaws scene with the father and son and their hands mimicking each other.

THE AGING COUPLE FEMALE, still trying to adjust something and release the fixture, chuckles.

The shade falls over to viciously kick THE AGING COUPLE FEMALE. . .

                    THE AGING COUPLE MALE
               You'll be finished soon and I
               will have your shade.

                    THE AGING COUPLE FEMALE
               Enough, I still need it. The
               others will arrive soon enough.

                    THE AGING COUPLE MALE
               You'd better hope so.

The bird glowers at THE AGING COUPLE MALE, then walks out.

INT./EXT. INDOOR CONCERT VENUE - NIGHT

The story begins with CARLA getting called in to attend a music event but for her to consider not going. The man who she is going to replace is another company representative and she is supposed to replace him. He attends the 8/16 concert but reneges at the last moment and has her go instead because she would have been called away from work to be with her family but decided to leave the kids with her husband instead. Her work is related to representing performers and subsequently making contract based recommendations therein.

The day is hot but the night is nice and cool.

INT. INDOOR CONCERT VENUE - NIGHT

                                              CONTINUED

[CUT AWAY]
>   MUSIC PERFORMER
>   So I hear there's a reviewer in
>   the audience! Where are you?
>   I'm not afraid of you!

Cheers all around.

>   MUSIC PERFORMER
>   Okay. When I say, 'How many,'
>   raise your hand if you are what
>   I describe: How many of you are
>   married? How many of you are
>   here on a date? How many of you
>   just realized you were here on
>   a date when the person sitting
>   next to you raised their hand?

Everyone laughs. A couple of people are surprised.

>   MUSIC PERFORMER
>   Just wanted to see how many
>   .   people get up.

[INAUDIBLE]
>   MUSIC PERFORMER
>   That joke is always funnier to
>   me than other people.

[END CUT AWAY]

MUSIC PERFORMER enters the stage (c-10). He is a comedian
and a producer, a multi-hyphenate. This person has also
worked in film production. With over 25 years in the
industry he has affiliation with both the Grammy's (The
Recording Academy) and the Oscar's (Academy of Motion
Picture Arts and Sciences). With one of his social media
accounts, he tipped the scales at 3.9 million followers
by 2013, and in the year after that he had 4 million. 5
years ago he had over 10 million followers and today he
has 13.1 M. He steps to the front of the stage and stands
in the center. In between songs the performer cuts away
from the music and segues into stand-up comedy.

CONTINUED

MUSIC PERFORMER sits on a wooden stool and rests one
one hand upon his thigh as he prepares to sing. There
is one water glass on the table beside him. A second
cup of water is brought to the stage. CONDUCTOR for the
orchestra moves his hands to motion the instruments in
tune. A gentle hum fills the air. Three violinists are
seated in the front row. A multitude of other instruments
such as the Piano, Guitar, Saxophone, and Cello to name
a few are grouped together in aisles situated nearby
the MUSIC PERFORMER. The musician is talking in between
sets. He walks to the front of the stage.

[INAUDIBLE]

                    MUSIC PERFORMER
               That joke is always funnier to
               me than other people.

                    AUDIENCE MEMBER 01
               This guy is great.

                    AUDIENCE MEMBER 02
               Omg. I love that song

                    AUDIENCE MEMBER 03
               Yeah

                    MUSIC PERFORMER
               So I hear there's a reviewer in
               the audience! Where are you?
               I'm not afraid of you!

When the music begins the overture stops for the MUSIC
PERFORMER to introduce the next song. He begins to sing
and a person stands up and walks through the back of
the audience. When the person returns to the audience,
one of the first songs is completed. A man on his phone
posts a picture of the event to his social media feed.

He performs a song, entitled "Old Man River" (c-16).

> MUSIC PERFORMER
> There has been some controversy
> over whether white performers
> should even sing that song. It's
> true because on one hand it is
> about the black experience and
> on the other hand it's in my key.

He takes a drink of water from the cup on the table
beside him. When he lifts the cup the illusion of two
cups (that) appear as one is the impression that is
created. The effect can only be seen from a specific
angle and so when the MUSIC PERFORMER picks up one glass
to take a drink that makes it look like it appears as
though either one of the two options listed below:

Option #1 the glass never left the table yet he holds
that very thing in his hand.
Option #2 the cup that is being lifted has never left
the table.

Applause all around. The MUSIC PERFORMER does an encore.

On the 8/16 show his hair is styled to the effect of
what it looks like at the turn of the century in some
interviews. When you look up close. Although from a
distance the style appears contemporary. He has a cute
little dimple at the curvature of the anterior front
side of the mandible.

"Every time I see him it's always like oh he got another
makeover" - Commentary on a quote from COWORKER and
The MUSIC PERFORMER in a 1999 time frame interview for
a TV Series

EXT. STREET ENTRANCE - NIGHT

Across the street in a different region is a bright
movie theater.

People in a movie theater texting in the front row. The
bright light from the screen flashing. Sometimes men
will fight to show their affection for a woman.

CONTINUED

ON THEATER SCREEN
Man punches other man.

FEMALE in audience with MALE clutches his arm and holds
him tight as they both watch the scene play out in front
of them in film.

People think it's entertainment on video.

But in real life, sometimes the thing we see on the
screen can have legal repercussions.

Trespassing - Breaking and entering a premises without
permission or consent.

Implied consent: If the premises allows access.

                        [CUT AWAY]

                    ANTAGONIST VILLAIN
                What was I supposed to think?

                       [END CUT AWAY]

Harassment - a person constantly commenting on
things that a person is doing and casting judgements
("officious") in a manner that is non-consensual.

Implied consent: If the person allows communication.

                        [CUT AWAY]

                    ANTAGONIST VILLAIN
                   (intent to cause harm)
                    She was asking for it.

                       [END CUT AWAY]

Assault - punching, spitting, kicking, touching physical
contact that is not consensual. When a person is asleep
they are legally unable to consent.

                                               CONTINUED

Implied consent: If the person allows physical contact.

                    [CUT AWAY]

                    ANTAGONIST VILLAIN
               I don't see any reason for a
               report.

                    [END CUT AWAY]

Stalking - following a person physically and finding out
where they live in order to assault, harass or trespass
with the intent to cause harm.

Implied consent: If the person makes their information
public.

                    [CUT AWAY]

                    ANTAGONIST VILLAIN
               I had a right.

                    [END CUT AWAY]

There are lots of reasons why people call the police.
Physically assaulting someone would be one of them.
Sometimes people think it's funny like entertainment.
And other times it can be more serious.

LAUREN and CHASE are the new happy couple.

He calls out. . .

                    ATTENDANT GUARD
               Hello. Excuse me. Stop.

CHASE, smiling, and LAUREN, surprised, stop.

Security footage at the movie theater shows a couple
being greeted. The ATTENDANT GUARD unlatches the metal
clasp that draws a partition from one side of the

entrance to the other. They happily enter the F-1 theater, the woman looking ahead as the man accompanies leading beside her.

Sometimes things just seem to work out on the first try.

And other times you need to wait before you try again.

BONUS #04 "DOWNTOWN CROSSING"

                    SUPPLEMENTAL OFFICER 01
                    His real name is Gary.

BUILDING MANAGER M-01 and BUILDING MANAGER M-02 stand
inside the room.

BUILDING MANAGER M-01, not happy, turns to exit...

                    BUILDING MANAGER M-01
                    What was she thinking?

BUILDING MANAGER M-01, his eyes concerned on the report...

                    BUILDING MANAGER F-01
                    He left a work notice with
                    BUILDING MANAGER M-02 the he
                    would return.

                    BUILDING MANAGER M-01
                    You both are fools to
                    believe him.

FADE TO BLACK:

FADE IN:

EXT. MAJOR RIVER - DAY

A storm weather front that is turbulent churns the
waters of the river, tossing branches and culling grime
in its wake.

Title: Twenty Years Later

INT. GYM: BELOW MAIN FLOOR: OFFICE - DAY

LEAD GYM MANAGER, in uniform, unblemished work order
in hand, stands alone in an office. The isolated white
background demonstrates his form in profile. A impossible

                                              CONTINUED

expression on his face. Beside him outside through an industrial grade glass composite window...

EXT. STREET: BELOW MAIN GYM FLOOR - DAY

HORSE 03, a large, grey, Appaloosa mare, calmly munches on cud from a feeding MOUNTED OFFICER F-02 has provided. There is one hand around her neck.

INT. GYM: BELOW MAIN FLOOR - DAY

Suddenly, the rope rises up and comes down hard, causing...

CHASE, looking blanched, to lunge too quickly, banging his knee on a low aerobic step as he hastens his way towards the mat.

EXT. STREET - DAY

LAUREN, dry heaving and confused, partitions her way through the racially diverse crowd of distracted, busy, pedestrians at the downtown crossing on the road at the end of the alley.

Standing at a side entrance, her heart skips a beat when she leans forward and vomits.

Wiping her mouth when finished, she stares at...

The muted notifications on her phone from CHASE.

A guy who liked the food is seen unaware of anything having transpired in the area behind him and where he is seated.

CONTINUED

BONUS #05 "INTERRUPTING"

EXT. APARTMENT COMPLEX - DAY

The RAID WORKER M-02 takes a bite of the sandwich as
he walks. He says nothing woman on the inside of the
entrance walks out to see what is happening, as another
vehicle pulls up a man walks in front of the scene.

The aging couple male is seated in a chair in the TV
room drinking a single malt. He is reading the newspaper
and watching TV (football sports) and as light shines in
to the home through an exterior window his wife is in
the kitchen, situated beneath an isolated light to the
side she is reading on. The gait of her body is tilted
forward as she is engrossed in reading the newspaper
one leg is extended outward at an angle. The darkness
of the day within the room is illuminated by the outside
light shining in which fresh rainfall that was pouring
earlier stopped, leaving behind beads of moisture on
each leaf in the plant life outside. That moisture would
then evaporate in the heat of the day. Leaving a weight
in the air that hung as if it were cast in the weather.

                    AGING COUPLE FEMALE
                    What is that sound?

                    AGING COUPLE MALE
            AGING COUPLE FEMALE, come back inside.

[AGING COUPLE MALE FLASHBACK]
"When I first found her. I tracked her." He said. "When
I found him, I chased him." She said. "I didn't know it
but she was doing the same thing! She was tracking me.
Oh, man. . . That first time, when I saw her walking
down the steps. That's when I knew my bachelor days were
over. But it wasn't until she sent me that recording of
"you belong to me." That's when I knew for sure." He said.

[END AGING COUPLE MALE FLASHBACK]

                                              CONTINUED

                    AGING COUPLE FEMALE
          Hey! Where are you going?
          You're going the wrong way!

                    AGING COUPLE MALE
          Come. She needs to rest.

                    RAID WORKER M-02
          (turns to RAID WORKER M-02)
          The building residents were
          notified.

INT. HALLWAY - DAY

                    RAID WORKER M-02
          This is the place.

                    MITCH 01
          Here we are.

                    RAID WORKER F-01
          Are we at the right place?

                    RAID WORKER M-01
          Yes.

                    RAID WORKER M-02
          This is the side they were
          talking about.

                    RAID WORKER F-01
          (beeps with the dispatch a code)

                    RAID WORKER M-03
          Why do we have to go this
          way on the other side of the
          building?

                    MITCH 01
          I know what you're thinking man.

                                        CONTINUED

There's another entrance in which officials Are approaching at the same time we have a warrant to apprehend evidence from this specific designation one of the workers in the crew.

RAID WORKER M-01, boastfully...

>   RAID WORKER M-01
>   And many have entered and
>   searched.

SERGEANT, combative, lowers his hand towards ANDREW...

>   RAID WORKER F-02
>   You answer my question, or
>   search by this system. That is
>   your choice.

RAID WORKER F-01 is too slow in reaching out to a now...

ANDREW, ...

>   ANDREW
>   I would rather search than be
>   responsible for a forced entry
>   by another.
>   So hold to your map

>   RAID WORKER M-03
>   (boastful)
>   They accept your warrant.

RAID WORKER M-01, resets his device, then casually, lowers the cover...

>   RAID WORKER M-01
>   That is your decision? So be it.

RAID WORKER M-02 stands beside MELODY and stares in complete surprise at BUILDING MANAGER 01 and BUILDING MANAGER 02...

                                        CONTINUED

                    BUILDING MANAGER 02
                Did he just open the side of
                the wall? I thought they were -

MATTHEW is not listening. He glares beyond BUILDING
MANAGER 01 as he pulls back his device.

RAID WORKER M-01, frustrated as he moves the barrier
aside, yells out to ANDREW...

                    BUILDING MANAGER 01
                Is this truly necessary?

MATTHEW, meaning to be officious, lowers his visor...

                        MITCH 01
                Ask him.

                        MATTHEW
                Ask her.

                        MELODY
                Ask him.

                        ANDREW
                He's the one with the familial
                trace.

Before RAID WORKER 01 can respond, both RAID WORKER
02 and MATTHEW walk towards one another. Their devices
pointed at the others destination. Inside of the wall
they find corroborative evidence. Among many things
including which a fob key that contains building access
points complete with time stamps.

EXT. COMPLEX PARKING LOT - DAY

                        ANDREW
                That car. I know that car. Who
                is driving it?

                                        CONTINUED

He urges his forensic scanner through the assemblage
of shrubbery.

                    MELODY
          Where the heck is Andrew going?

All, befuddled, look to ANDREW.

ANDREW stares down BUILDING MANAGER. . .

                    ANDREW
          You there on the apse. . . hold.

                  RAID WORKER #3
          That's the company's vehicle.

MAINTENANCE ASSISTANT (PATSY), surprised, looks towards
ANDREW then quickly away. His jacket falls slightly to
reveal his face.

                  TECHNICIAN
          Is he that guy?

MAINTENANCE ASSISTANT (PATSY) anxiously drives the
vehicle to a start.

ANDREW whistles and the vehicle stops.

MAINTENANCE ASSISTANT (PATSY) tries to get the vehicle
to move forward.

The vehicle, indignant, spins and rears, moving
quickly. . .

MAINTENANCE ASSISTANT (PATSY) exits backwards to hit
his head on the ground. A mighty collision but it is...

EXT. COUNTY JAIL - MOMENTS LATER

The next scene is for the long term parking lot.

                                        CONTINUED

There is a moment to show the villain being taken to
jail after attacking a young woman who lives in the
area at the same time the dispatch counter has received
numerous reports that indicate an abandoned vehicle in
the long-term parking lot of the airport.

2 HOURS LATER

INT. PRECINCT DISATCH COUNTER - AFTERNOON

The dispatch counter is buzzing with incoming reports.

                    DISPATCH COUNTER
               I don't see any reason for a
               report.

ANDREW, incredulous. . .

                    ANDREW [V.O]
               The vehicle being parked there
               for less than 2 weeks? That's
               what it took for him to file
               this report?

CADET #1 and CADET #2 scoff.

EXT. DOWNTOWN PRECINCT: DISPATCH DESK - NIGHT

                    MITCH 01
               (cigarette gesture)
               Huh

                    ANDREW
               What's this

                    CADET
               He keeps trying to file a
               report about this abandoned
               vehicle at the long term
               parking lot of the airport but
               the vehicle hasn't been there

                                        CONTINUED

> long enough to constitute it
> being abandoned.

ANDREW is interrupted while speaking to MITCH 01
about the long term parking lot at the airport. Their
conversation is interrupted with a report of a woman
being assaulted. She is physically assaulted while
walking in a crowded area.

CONTINUED

BONUS #06 "BIRD 01, BIRD 02"

Moral Lesson: A bird in the hand is worth two in the
bush (a-02). A bird is seated beside a person in the
kitchen who is cooking. On a perch, the winged bird is
a domesticated parrot whose feathers are not clipped.
Parrots look funny when they are just sitting there at
rest. Their beak is in a constant stable curvature. The
form is like this creepy smile that is permanent. Like
vaudeville from a time when things that are totally fake
but made for show back then BUT are transparent today.

The way a bird looks when it takes a huge bite of
sunflower seeds is fascinating. Astounded, the bird
holds fast its feet in one place tacked down to its perch
by its own impetus. Leaning back, the birds circles its
core and goes back in for another bite.

                    DOMESTICATED PARROT OWNER
                    Honey Bun, you want some more
                    food? The bird looks at its
                    owner, expectantly.

                    DOMESTICATED PARROT
                    "Drop it! Hungry!"

Birds need to eat every 25 minutes because of how fast
their metabolism is. The owner turns away from the table
and stands. Walking from one room into another like an
animal in the water beside it the human walks by as
the bird engorges its feathers showing a full wingspan
on display.

INT. BIRD CAGE - DAY

There are two birds in the cage, BIRD 01 and BIRD 02.
The cage door opens due to a faulty hinge. The bird
flies out. And that is followed by the other one. BIRD
01 returns to the cage and BIRD 02 clings to side of the
house and looks around at the trees which surround the
area. BIRD 02 escapes and subsequently flies through
multiple areas.

                                        CONTINUED

[KEY FRAME: "APEX PREDATOR" TAKE 01] INT. MAIN HOUSE –
DAY CAT 02 is in the lobby of the home and is looking
outside and sees BIRD 02 doing a fly by outside.

[END KEY FRAME: "APEX PREDATOR" TAKE 01] [FLASHBACK]
HOMEMAKER F-01 is in the kitchen baking food.

HUSBAND M-01 is in the office with MAN-20 when he hears
the sound of the bird cage door open and that's when the
birds, BIRD 01 and BIRD 02, they both fly out. The moment
in the office after the birds escape is punctuated by
the image of two men reading something on the desktop.
The door to the office opens and a dark on the desktop.
The door to the office opens and dark haired woman
wearing glasses knocks as she enters the room.

                    HOMEMAKER F-01
              The birds got out.

                         MAN 20
              What?

                      HUSBAND M-01
              How?

[KEY FRAME: "APEX PREDATOR" TAKE 02] CAT 02 sees the
BIRD 02 and is like all crouching tiger hidden dragon
at the sight of it. He won't have a go at it cause on
account of he being inside and all. [END KEY FRAME:
"APEX PREDATOR" TAKE 02]

                         CAT 02
              (thumps paws on the carpet)
              [END FLASHBACK]
              CAT 02 sees the BIRD 02 and
              is like all crouching tiger
              hidden dragon at the sight of
              it. He won't have a go at it
              cause on account of he being
              inside and all.

EXT. WOODS - DAY

                                          CONTINUED

There is a sign that says no vehicles beyond this point. The shadow of a bird flies overhead obscured into the shape of rapid moving clouds. There are no shadows in the sky.

EXT. INVESTIGATION SITE: EMBANKEMENT - DUSK

> FIRST RESPONDER M-01
> The sun is low in the sky.

MITCH 01 and MITCH 02 ["MARK") aimlessly move the materials arm in arm they walk together where MATTHEW approaches them in a clearing of the investigation site, the sim card, cell phones and a large encasement box.

They stop, becoming serious, stare into one another's eyes, then begin to open the encasement.

INT. DOWNTOWN PRECINCT: HALLWAY - NIGHT

A size 000 silhouette walks in the hall inside. The form pauses momentarily at a door, then disappears.

INT. DOWNTOWN PRECINCT: ME ROOM - NIGHT

The soft profile of the LEAD MEDICAL EXAMINER and ME DEPARTMENT HEAD carefully un-entwine somatic evidence on a table of microscope slides. MEDICAL ASSISTANT M-01 and Medical Assistant M-02 prepare the forensic machine.

> ME DEPARTMENT HEAD
> See? You press the skin and
> if there's white that turns
> pink that means the skin is
> healthy. There's no reaction.

> MEDICAL ASSISTANT M-01
> (nods)

EXT. RURAL COUNTRYSIDE - DAWN

                              CONTINUED

The sun rising behind the distant city can be seen from the mountains.

MOUNTED OFFICER F-01, on her HORSE 01, glares steadfastly at the embankment. She then turns to the MOUNTED OFFICER M-01 on HORSE 02 and they ride away. Glancing back several times over her shoulder, MOUNTED OFFICER M-01 leads them away from the site.

EXT. NEARBY HOME: DRIVEWAY - DAY

HOMEMAKER F-01 sits reading a breaking news update on her phone under the shade of a tree beside the garage. She suddenly frowns and two people, a MOTHER 01 and CHILD 01 appear to her side.

Helping her, they present an innovation in chip technology: The domesticated animal chip that allows for ping data tracking is that BIRD 02 has a microchip which appears on a phone when reset as if it were mobile device. The only crux of this innovation is what happens when it goes out of range. BIRD 02 is very fragile.

EXT. CITY OF THE RURAL HOME - DAWN

The sound of birds at morning light.

INT. NEARBY HOME: OFFICE - DAWN

The cries of a bird heard in the early morning.

Smiling proudly, HOMEMAKER F-01 holds a chirping parrot to her breast.

BIRD 01 is inside the cage when HUSBAND M-01 opens the latched door and places the parrot's mate, BIRD 02, back inside the cage. BIRD 02 stands on the perch affectionately beside BIRD 01 and is cooing softly as the parrots are reunited.

CONTINUED

BONUS #07 "AIRPORT TERMINAL"

The Airport Scenes open with the guy who misses his flight:
EXTRA MAN 05 who misses his flight. And is seated in BAR AREA 01 and he has a drink in front of him and a donut. He is checking out EXTRA WOMAN 02 who is in the SEATING AREA 01.
EXTRA ANDREW STUNT DOUBLE trying to download something on his phone.
EXTRA MOTHER 01 and CHILD 01 at news stand looking for FATHER 01.
EXTRA WOMAN 01 argues at TICKET COUNTER 01.
EXTRA WOMAN 02 talking on phone in SEATING AREA 01. An object presses between an airline ticket (c-25) and a beige plastic rectangle in the cylindrical shape of an ellipse displayed a small, metallic (d-25) square shaped flat container. The heel of her platform shoe breaks.
EXTRA CHILD 02 and EXTRA CHILD 03 whining and complaining.
EXTRA MAN 04 looking for EXTRA MAN 03 "Bogart" Story.
EXTRA The PASSENGERS 01-04 story leading to content associated with THE LONG TERM PARKING LOT and reports of an abandoned vehicle to "How They Got the Court Order" Story.

PROPS: Hard Drink Bar Display and Soft Drink/Coffee and Restaurant display. Newspaper and Magazine Rack beside Candy and Snacks.

INT./EXT. AIRPORT TERMINAL - DAY

The Passengers find each other in the Airport Terminal but there is a crux where one of the two parties get sent back to the parking lot where they need to get a motel. That's when they (PASSENGER 01 AND PASSENGER 02) after the TICKET COUNTER 01 Scene, PASSENGER 01 and PASSENGER 02 return the next day after locating a motel to spend the night for the duration of their layover. The Palm Springs Couple find a note on their car from the Parking lot Security guard. PASSENGER 01 reads the note: "Just a notice that you've been parked here too long." Signed, the long term parking lot ATTENDANT. His wife, PASSENGER 02 is all like "next time we're going to Florida." (d-02)

INT. AIRPORT TERMINAL: TICKET COUNTER 01 - DAY

The FLIGHT ATTENDANT'S eyes go suddenly wide with astonishment as...

PASSENGER 01 raises his oversize luggage, spins and separates the grip tie.

PASSENGER 02 picks up the separated grip tie. She hands it to...

PASSENGER 01, deep in focus, as he binds a new grip tie unbroken. He mutters to himself in a low voice...

                    PASSENGER 01
          Where   is   the   AIRPORT   BUS
          DRIVER? Where might he be?

He opens a zipper into the exterior hem of his luggage, then attaches the unbroken tie.

                    PASSENGER 01
          PASSENGER 03, you will ride to
          the D FLIGHT DECK.
          PASSENGER 02, you to FLIGHT
          DECK D-03. I will ride to the
          parking lot with PASSENGER 01.

PASSENGER 03 and PASSENGER 04 turn to leave. They are stopped by -

                    PASSENGER 01
          There's no time to get food. I
          know you wanted to grab lunch
          before the flight.

PASSENGER 02, apprehensive...

                                        CONTINUED

                    PASSENGER 02
          If   we   should,   instead   of
          getting a new flight, go on
          standby for an open flight -

PASSENGER 01 rises irritated to his full height. He
quickly composes the luggage...

                    PASSENGER 01
          If you catch an earlier flight -
          do not worry about luggage.
          I will make a follow up call
          to the airport myself.

PASSENGER 03 and PASSENGER 04 nodding, then quickly
walk away.

                    PASSENGER 01
          PASSENGER 04'S son will
          pay for upgrade
          services.
          But first - I will get layover
          arrangements
          For us at a motel.

EXT. LONG TERM PARKING LOT - DAY

ATTENDANT not paying attention to the vehicles around
him, untangles the wires from the boot lock bound at
his feet. The wheel laying beside it.

                                        CONTINUED

BONUS #08 "LIVE STREAMING VIDEO"

Checks time on watch. Inbound train crossing the high
speed rail to segue Carla back in.

INT. INBOUND TRAIN - MORNING

A MOTHER applies SPF 20 hand moisturizer to CHILD'S
unblemished upper side of the hand.

CHILD tries to curb their enthusiasm.

                    MOTHER
          It concerns me to see you ride
          in without sunblock.

                    A BUSINESSMAN
          (on the phone)
          It's fine. The stock exchange
          is working.

                    CARLA
          (on the phone)
          But the poor cell phone signal
          is not helping.

                    TEENAGER 01
          Trust me. This next stop is
          ours.

                    TEENAGER 02
          It'll be totally fine.

MOTHER stops talking at the reaction from CHILD. When
the train approaches their stop. She starts to put away
the sunblock...

EXT. HANK DRIVING CAR - MORNING

                    HANK
          You look just like your mother.

                                        CONTINUED

                         JACOB
               Okay Dad.

                         BRADEN
               Drop us off here, Dad!

EXT. SCHOOL GROUNDS - DAY

HANK leaves a knife out on the table where he forgets
to pack the kids lunches. They are driving to school.
The vehicle pulls up to the curb and the kids get out.
BRADEN and JACOB are greeted by CROSSING GUARD and a
TEACHER.

                         TEACHER
                    No classes will be cancelled
                    they think the good weather
                    is staying here. It's in the
                    weather report. They're not
                    going to cancel the ice cream
                    social.

He holds up a hand to show his phone with the weather
Application open to silence any protest from the CROSSING
GUARD...

                         TEACHER
                    My phone is right. You should
                    take a day off. It will help.

                         CROSSING GUARD
                    I won't argue. I can see that
                    it won't do any good to worry.
                    Have a nice day.

EXT. COUNTRY RAIL ROAD - DAY

The five TRAIN PASSENGERS exit and walk away from the
platform.

INT. INBOUND TRAIN - DAY

                                           CONTINUED

CARLA stops to look up. There were a lot of windows
open on her phone. In order to navigate to the website
for supplemental information about the live streaming
concert being streamed she would have to close a window.
But not all live streaming has the same feed. The
presentation would differ from one platform server as
compared to another. There was an interesting comment
that appeared as an additional message that was followed
by another comment. That was live video streaming. The
motion of the train chugging along past the river across
from NE Englewood. She is viewing content about the
recent concert that she attended. Carla is streaming
this live video per the request of her current employer,
a field that is in the Media and Entertainment industry.

[SOCIAL MEDIA STARTS A LIVE VIDEO]

The MUSIC PERFORMER looks down at phone on table beside
him. He sits in the foreground and comments to the other
performers in his band.

                    MUSIC PERFORMER
          I'm gonna check the feed. Woah,
          I'm seeing a lot of emoticons
          and upper case.

                    AUDIENCE POSTING
          YEEEEEAAAHHHHH

                    AUDIENCE POSTING
          Great show.

                    AUDIENCE POSTING
          Has anyone seen my remote
          control?

                    AUDIENCE POSTING
          This is the BEST

                    AUDIENCE POSTING
          The computer feed is behind.

                                        CONTINUED

                    AUDIENCE POSTING
          Sing, This song.

                    MUSIC PERFORMER
          It's just us there's no one
          here. It's just the internet.

                    AUDIENCE POSTING
          You got this!

                    MUSIC PERFORMER
          I know.

                    LIVE AUDIENCE
               [INAUDIBLE]

                    MUSIC PERFORMER
          What

The music is in between songs on the live streaming
video while performers are talking during halftime on
another LIVE VIDEO STREAM.

[END SOCIAL MEDIA STARTS A LIVE VIDEO]

INT. INBOUND TRAIN - DAY

                    SMS ALERT GRAPHIC
               (blocks screen)
               AT-20 NAME

On the train, A man on his phone posts a picture of the
event to his social media feed.

On the train, a man watches the sports channel and has
the volume on his electronic device turned up without
headphones.

On the train, a man enters a pin from his credit card
to check the status of a recent payment that had gone
through and was paid to see if whether or not it was

                                        CONTINUED

paid. A video interview is streaming in the background. Several seats away Carla readjusts the earbud headphones that attach to the headset wire of her smart phone device.

On the train, a group of people wait to exit at a stop 1 hr. 20 minutes into the commute.

On the train, Carla is seated. She struggles to stay cool but the airflow fan doesn't work.

INT./EXT. INBOUND TRAIN: CABIN - DAY

CARLA watches, anxiously from below, videos pile their attachments onto user profiles and playlists. She sees other passengers making preparations to exit on the next stop taking place.

She motions behind her seat and the ATTENDANT appears.

>   the ATTENDANT
>   Are you able to find everything
>   you need?

>   CARLA
>   I'm not sure. But I'd like to
>   try and get some fresh air
>   flow.

CARLA looks to the nearby ATTENDANT...

>   CARLA
>   This one doesn't work but
>   now the one in this seat is
>   working.

She turns back away from the ATTENDANT...

>   ATTENDANT
>   (to another passenger)
>   Do you have everything you
>   need?

                                        CONTINUED

                          PASSEGER
                    Yes. Thank you.

                          ATTENDANT
                    Okay

                          PASSENGER
                    (on phone)
                    Remember that thing I told
                    you? I meant it.

CONTINUED

BONUS #09 "REGIONAL ALERT SYSTEM"

The screen on Carla's phone darkens. She switches away
from the live streaming event to view a pre-recorded
video posting on a similar video site that her potential
employer wants her to review. Because she has 500+ search
engine pages open she would have to close another page
in order to open this new one. She closes one page and
openes another, when a repeat of the same emergency text
appeared at the top of the screen and a few comments
appear at the bottom of the frame. Another emergency
text appears at the top of the screen again and it is
the same alert with the same code.

                    SMS ALERT GRAPHIC
                  (blocks screen)
                  AT-20 NAME

The alert sound is heard on the phones of the people on
the live television set at the same time it is heard on
the phones of the people in the train car.

The sound reverberates like a ripple effect.

                    SMS ALERT GRAPHIC
                  (blocks screen)
                  AT-20 NAME

A man watching the sports channel is talking out loud
to the screen. On this sports channel, there is a man
depicted in the frame on someone's cellphone screen. On
the screen this man who is live looks down at his phone
and then faces away from the camera when a person off
stage made an illegible comment.

                    MAN 1 BACKSTAGE
                  Did you see that alert?

                    MAN 2 ON STAGE
                  Is this the same alert that
                  has been going off all day?

                                              CONTINUED

                    MAN 2 BACKSTAGE
          Yeah.

MAN 1 BACKSTAGE holds a phone up facing in profile toward
MAN 2 ON STAGE

                    SMS ALERT GRAPHIC
                (blocks screen)
                AT-20 NAME

A person across the aisle says something.

Another person does not say anything.

Someone looks down at their phone.

INT. INBOUND TRAIN: NEW YORK CITY - DAY

The screen freezes on CARLA's phone. The live stream
gets truncated and a corporate note from the sponsor
appears and the screen freezes again. She presses the
rewind button. The screen on her phone brightens. And a
text from HANK comes in which she discounts for a moment
because she assumes that it is another emergency alert
text message notification that appears on her screen.
CARLA sighs and turns off the live feed and returns to
a buffered video interview of the PRODUCER who is the
same person as the MUSIC PERFORMER in the previous LIVE
VIDEO STREAM.

                    SMS [HANK)
               When the kids get home, I'm
               going to the market.

                    SMS [CARLA]
           . . .

                    SMS [HANK]
           Do you need anything?

                    SMS [CARLA]
           . . .

                                              CONTINUED

                    SMS [HANK]
. . .

                    SMS [CARLA]
Bread

                    SMS [HANK]
I told the kids they could walk
home from the bus. It isn't
even raining here yet.

                    SMS [CARLA]
Did you see the severe weather
alert?

                    SMS (HANK]
Yeah.

                    SMS [CARLA]
What were you thinking.

                    SMS [HANK]
What?

            SMS ALERT GRAPHIC
(blocks screen)
AT-20 NAME

                    SMS [CARLA)
They can't walk home from the
bus stop. I don't like it when
you do this.

                    SMS [HANK]
It's fine.

                    SMS [CARLA]
Really? Because the last time
I checked Braden thinks it's
okay to talk to strangers.

                                        CONTINUED

                   SMS ALERT GRAPHIC
          (blocks screen)
          AT-20 NAME

                    SMS [HANK]
          We've gone over this.

                   SMS [CARLA]
          Look, I'm just saying.

                    SMS [HANK]
          What if something happens?
          They need to be able to ask
          for help.

                   SMS [CARLA]
          Call you later.

                   SMS ALERT GRAPHIC
          (blocks screen)
          AT-20 NAME

                                              CONTINUED

BONUS #10 "TALK SHOW TV"

CARLA navigates away from the page and back to the
interview with the MUSIC PERFORMER who is also a PRODUCER
and presses the play button and looks down. The video
that she is viewing resumes.

INT. INBOUND TRAIN - DAY

The man on the video playing on the phone screen leans
forward, laughing, and presses his left hand to his
furrowed brow. The HOST laughs. He stops talking and
glances up. He holds both hands up and uses the index
and middle fingers of each hand to make air quotes.
He shifts the focus back to the MUSIC PERFORMER who
is also a PRODUCER. CARLA presses the stop button. The
screen fades to black, and a row of search options
appear in the middle of the video frame. The screen on
her phone brightens. The live streaming video resumes.
The video that is playing pauses. When she presses the
play button, the screen begins to load. CARLA focuses
her eyes and stares down at the link. The orbital icon
of the cursor shifts in circles, which begin to rotate
counterclockwise.

The video begins to play and CARLA listens through
earbuds. Her eyes focus on the air outside, above the
train car, and she looks back down to the video that is
playing. The screen is black at first, and then three
people, two men and a woman, are shown sitting at a
table. In the next scene a man appears. In between the
two men sits the woman, wearing a purple shirt. Both
men wear black. All three of them have black mugs. The
audience applauds.

                          HOST
                    (gestures and laughs)
                    And that brings us to, uh,
                    the controversy. And I really
                    appreciate you for bringing a
                    controversy onto our show for
                    our season premiere.

                                            CONTINUED

The HOST leans forward and looks directly at his guest,
who is the MUSIC PERFORMER who is also a PRODUCER of the
show. He opens both hands outward and faces the other
side of the table, where the MUSIC PERFORMER who is also
a PRODUCER (GUEST) is seated.

                    GUEST
          Yes.

                    HOST
          It is very good for ratings.

                    GUEST
          Yes, I-

                    HOST
          You could have talked about it
          on other shows all week.

                    GUEST
          Yes, but I saved it for you.

                    HOST
          Oh, and you saved it for us.
          And if you don't know what's
          going on, you probably haven't
          been watching the news. But
          let's show you what happened on
          his show Sunday night, which
          was hysterical, as always.

There is a pause and both guests nod. The screen cuts
away to a clip from the controversial episode.

                    HOST
          This guy. This guy who did this
          is a hater. When people like
          that do what they do, I think
          you have to call them out.

They stop talking moments before laughter fills the air.
They nod in unison with his words and he looks away from

                                        CONTINUED

the camera. The scene switches back to the main stage
where MUSIC PERFORMER who is also the PRODUCER (GUEST)
is seated. The audience is laughing in astonishment.

> HOST
> I've got to call you out. Hey,
> I've got to call you out.

> GUEST
> Must be doing something right.

> HOST
> She is the queen of fake
> outrage. Whether it's another
> talk show host or you.

> GUEST
> Yeah. Always got to be somebody.

> SMS ALERT GRAPHIC
> (blocks screen)
> AT-20 NAME

CARLA closes the text message application and re-opens
the video streaming device.

The video that she is viewing resumes.

The HOST makes a gesture with both his hands that mimic
the action of spreading a deck of cards. The MUSIC
PERFORMER who is also a PRODUCER (GUEST) uses his hands
to mimic a row of dominoes falling.

She pauses the video and returns to the live video
stream closes the window.

CARLA turns the phone screen off.

One hour later the train arrives at the station.

CONTINUED

It is cold on the train. The chill in the air made her
chest have a slight trill. The afternoon light breaks
through the buildings as the train approaches the outer
perimeter of the city.

It is now midday. There is some scattered rain showers
and sun. In the city nearby there is a man rowing his
boat. It glided across the top of the water. Joggers
and people riding their bikes move along the pavement.

Birds fly overhead. Some in the flock swoop low in
horizontal form next to the train that is casting a
shadow against the ground. The river spreads out in a
mass expanse along the city and then draws into other
industrial and more suburban regions in the rural
countryside of the state. The sun sinks brightly against
the sprawling landscape.

EXT. NEW YORK CITY: DOWNTOWN MANHATTAN - DAY

RECORDING AGENT, in brand new jacket, waits with
ASSISTANT.

ASSISTANT looks up to her.

                    ASSISTANT
               (low voice)
          Hands off the fabric. (e-01)

RECORDING AGENT gently pats the fabric...

                    CARLA
          I'm sure we'll get along fine.

                    SMS ALERT GRAPHIC
               (blocks screen)
               AT-20 NAME

A man on his phone in one hand, while holding a bag of
groceries in the other nearby across the length of the
street, pressed a button on his phone.

                                        CONTINUED

                    SMS ALERT GRAPHIC
               (blocks screen)
               AT-20 NAME

A cellphone beeps. There is a regional alert that had
been continuously sent to her phone. But is it really
the regional alert system notification that the missing
woman had been found? The other day while driving and
the GPS monitor switched the background panel skin from
day to night an electronic billboard had that same kind
of alert.

                    SMS ALERT GRAPHIC
               C490-01 Missing Person. Info
               Please call 895-5555

                                           CONTINUED

COMING ATTRACTIONS:

INDEX FOR "SCREENPLAY"
RELEASE DATE: TBA Bibliography, First Edition.

1-100

82. The laser feature innovation helicopter on page _ _ _
83. The equestrian Department on page _ _ _
84. The "No Access" Region of the Conservatory on page _ _ _
85. The "Love" Theme Interviews and Documentary of Stories on page _ _ _
86. The profile of music performer structure on page _ _ _
87. The little guy who scares off the big guy only to turn around and see an even bigger guy behind him (d-03) on page _ _ _
88. The "Monster" theme by the music performer who is also a producer reference on page _ _ _
89. The Talk Show References on page _ _ _
90. The Social Media Reference on page _ _ _
91. The TV show Reference on page _ _ _
92. The Satellite TV Reference on page _ _ _
93. "The Value of a Dollar" Quotes on page _ _ _
94. The ATM Series on page _ _ _
95. The Persecution and Resulting Error on page _ _ _
96. The "Write Back" Audience on page _ _ _
97. Define "Ghosting" on page _ _ _
98. Define "Stratiation" on page _ _ _
99. Define "Catfishing" in both Antagonist and Protagonist Form on page _ _ _
100. Define "Anacathartic" on page _ _ _

Printed in the United States
by Baker & Taylor Publisher Services